THE SUPER RED RACER

Junior Discovers Work

by **Dave Ramsey**

Collect all of the *Junior's Adventures* books!

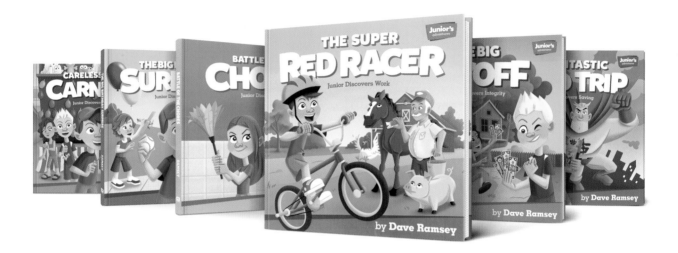

The Super Red Racer: Junior Discovers Work
© 2015 Lampo Licensing, LLC
Published by Ramsey Press, The Lampo Group, Inc.
Brentwood, TN 37027

For more information on Dave Ramsey, visit daveramsey.com or call 888.227.3223.

Editors: Amy Parker, Jen Gingerich
Project Management: Preston Cannon, Bryan Amerine and Mallory Darcy
Illustrations: Greg Hardin, John Trent and Kenny Yamada
Art Direction: Luke LeFevre, Brad Dennison and Chris Carrico

DEDICATION

Denise is my firstborn child—the first one Sharon and I had to teach to WORK for the things she wants in life. She has taught us so much about teaching children to work, and now watching her as an adult, we see the benefits of training your child well!

Thank you, Denise, for being such a wonderful daughter and for applying these life principles.

Love, Dad (Dave)

Early one Saturday morning, Junior crept out of bed and down the stairs. Saturday was the one day of the week when his parents could sleep in. He poured a gigantic bowl of cereal, plopped down on the couch, and flipped on the TV.

"Yesss!" Junior exclaimed, sending cereal flying. He was just in time to catch his favorite superhero, Dollar Bill, duking it out with the Credit Creep in *The Adventures of Dollar Bill*.

Junior's eyes were glued to the screen when up flashed
the coolest, most awesome
bike he had ever seen.
It was a Super Red Racer.
And it was only $79.

Oh, the things he could
do on a Super Red Racer!

Junior bounded up the stairs,
flung open the door to his room, and ran for his piggy bank.

Clinkity, clankity, clunk!
He shook that little pig until every last cent covered the bed.

"Eight dollars and forty-nine cents," he announced as he wrinkled his brow. "How am I ever going to get that Super Red Racer?"

Then, Junior had an idea.

"Dad," he whispered. "Daa-AD . . . DAD!"

"Erm hmmmph," Dad answered. One eye tried to open.

"Hey, Dad!" Junior took a deep breath. "So I was watching TV and Dollar Bill and Credit Creep were like, POW! Then there was this Super Red Racer with handlebar grips and silver spokes and pegs, and it's on sale for only $79, and I only have like $8, so I was thinking that maybe, well, will you and Mom buy it for me? Please?"

Dad's one eye was fully open now. "That's a lot of money, Junior," he said through a yawn. "And it's not in the budget to buy something we don't really need."

Junior lowered his head. "Awww. But Daaaaad?"

"Sorry, bud. It's just not in the budget," Dad answered.

"Yes, sir," Junior mumbled and shuffled out of the room.

Junior plopped back down on the couch just as the Credit Creep was running far, far away.

"Remember," Dollar Bill said, "the best place to go when you need money is to work!"

"That's it!" Junior jumped up and pointed at the TV. "Thank you, Dollar Bill!"

Junior stood at the end of his parents' bed with work boots on his feet and work gloves on his hands. "Dad! Mom! I am going to work!"

This time, his dad sat up in bed. "To where?"

"Whhasssumphh," mumbled his mom.

"To work!" Junior exclaimed again.
"Dollar Bill says that's where you go
when you need money."

"And he's right," Dad agreed, rubbing his eyes. "So where are you
  going to work?"

"Farmer Falzetti has chickens to feed and cows to milk. I'm going to
  start there."

"Well then . . . " Dad smiled. "Go to work!"

Junior walked over the hill to the farmhouse and called
through the screen door, "Farmer Falzetti?"

"Hey there, Junior!" Farmer Falzetti said as he opened the door.
"How can I help ya?"

"Well, there's this Super Red Racer bike that I really want . . ."

"Say no more." Farmer Falzetti smiled a knowing smile. "I could sure use some help around here, and I'd be happy to pay you for it. We'll call it a win-win deal."

"Yes, sir!" Junior grinned.

"Working on a farm is pretty hard work, ya know. What do you think you can do?"

"Well, I could feed the chickens and help with the horses and—"

Farmer Falzetti laughed. "Junior, have you ever groomed a horse?"

"Well, no sir, but I know I can learn."

"All right, son." Farmer Falzetti pulled on his boots and headed toward the barn with Junior close behind him. "You come Saturday mornings and every day after school, and I'll pay you $5 a day."

Junior nodded quickly as he calculated. Five dollars times six days is $30 a week. In just three weeks, he could have that Super Red Racer!

An explosion of feathers
and flapping flew in Junior's face.

"Help meee!" Junior yelled.

Squaaaaawk!

"Aw, they'll settle down in a minute." Farmer Falzetti grabbed a metal bucket and scooped up some feed. "Here chick, chick, chick."

The chickens pecked at the ground and at Junior's feet. "Whoa!" He laughed. "You've got to keep your feet moving fast around here!"

"What is that smell?" Junior asked when they got close to the feeding trough.

"Pig slop!" the farmer answered. "Mrs. Falzetti puts all the leftovers in this bucket. Then we add a little sour milk and use it to feed the pigs."

Junior took the bucket with one hand, held his nose with the other, and poured in the gooey concoction. The pigs came running.

Squeeeeeaal! Oink, oink, oink!

Then Junior followed Farmer Falzetti into the barn.

"Blaze," the farmer said to the reddish-brown horse, "Junior will be helping me groom you, so be nice." Farmer Falzetti slid a brush on his hand and gave one to Junior. "Ol' Blaze here loves a good brushing. Just don't get behind him."

Junior gently ran his brush down the horse's side, smoothing his hair, then began untangling his mane. Blaze blew a puff of air through his nostrils and nuzzled Junior with his head. Farmer Falzetti laughed. "Blaze says he's happy to meet you, Junior."

Every day after school, Junior went to the farm.

He fed the chickens, keeping his feet moving fast.

He slopped the pigs, holding the bucket in one hand and his nose with the other.

He brushed Blaze and gave him fresh hay.

Every Saturday morning when Junior finished, Farmer Falzetti paid him $30. And every Saturday when he got home, Junior counted his money.

The first week: $38.49!

The second week: $68.49!

And finally, after his third full week: $98.49!

Junior beamed as he counted out his money for the cashier at the toy store. And Dad was beaming right along with him.

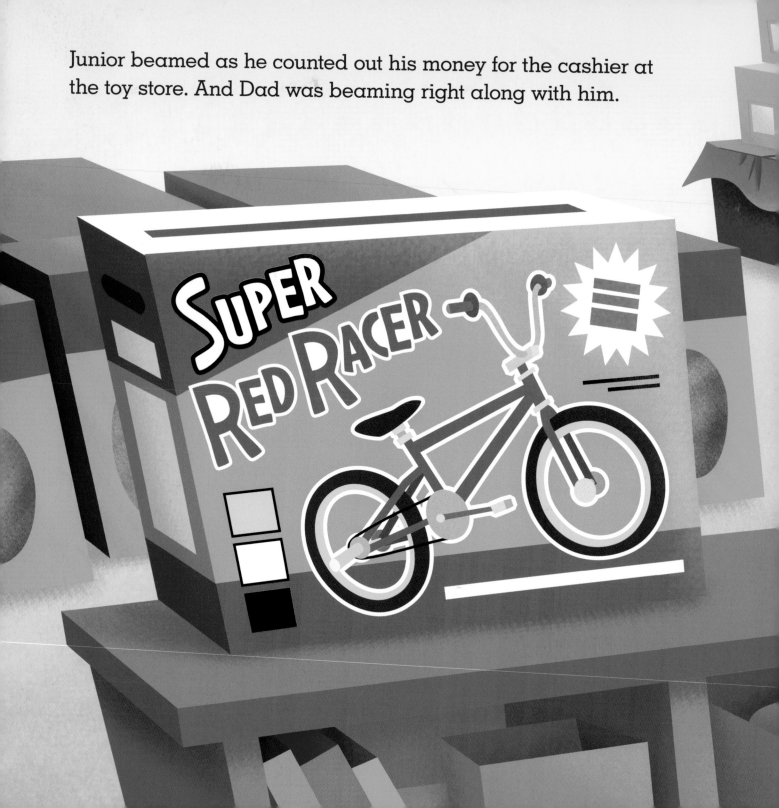

"I am so proud of you, Junior," Dad said as he tightened the last screw on the handlebars. "You knew what you wanted and did what you needed to get it."

"Yep, Dad." Junior grinned. "It's true that the best place to go when you need money is to work!"

And with that, Junior sped away on his Super Red Racer.